GREAT GRANDPA Loves me!

We're working on an app! Join us now & get it for free when we launch.

Unlimited illustrated children's stories like this one that teach **your** values (family, perseverance, courage, kindness, and much more) in one app including animations, music, read aloud, and even an option to insert familiar family faces into the story!

Once in a forest, deep in the woods,
Where animals played as animals should,
There was a wise and gentle bear,
A great-grandfather with silvery hair.

He had tender eyes of deepest blue,
And a smile that was always kind and true.
Great Grandpa Bear had much to say,
With words to brighten even cloudy days.

Early one morning, with sunshine bright,
His curious great-grandchild came into sight.
Darling Little Cub, with golden brown fur trim,
Appeared around the corner and ran straight to him!

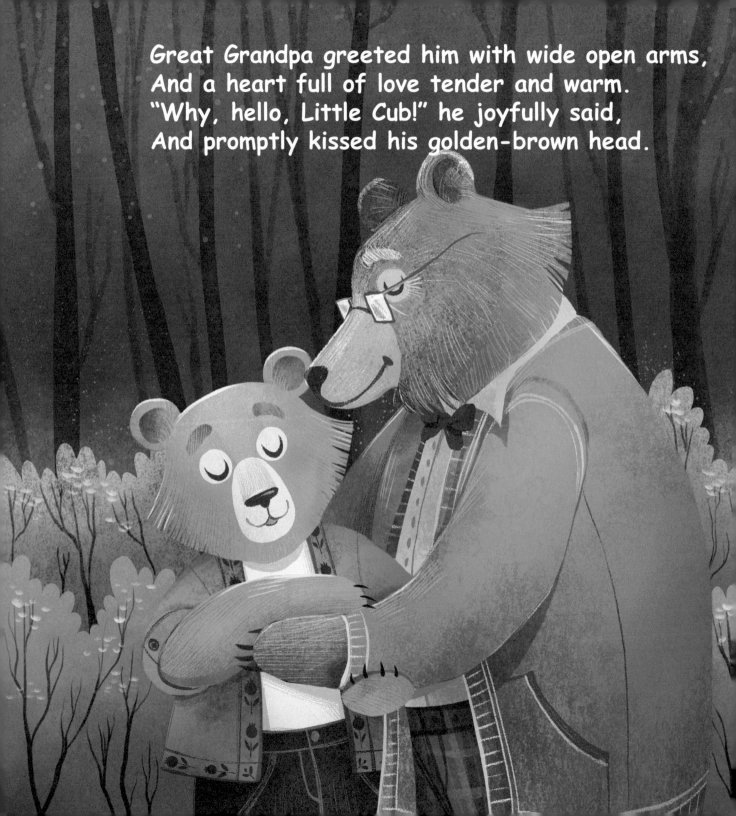

Great Grandpa greeted him with wide open arms,
And a heart full of love tender and warm.
"Why, hello, Little Cub!" he joyfully said,
And promptly kissed his golden-brown head.

"Let's go explore!" he shouted with glee,
For there was always so much to do and see!
Together, they loved roaming the woods,
Every adventure was exciting and good.

"Look," whispered Great Grandpa, pointing up high,
"The birds are soaring in the distant sky.
Their feathers are gleaming shiny and bright,
Oh, how colorful! What a delight!"

Little Cub's eyes widened like the moon,
As he watched them fly and heard their tune.
"Why do birds fly?" he asked again.
Great Grandpa answered with a knowing grin.

"They fly because they were given wings,
Just like you and I were given things...
Paws to walk along the ground,
And voices to make bear-like sounds."

"I like to talk!" Little Cub shouted.
"Yes, I know," Great Grandpa touted.
He nudged him along with sweet affection,
As Little Cub ran in a new direction.

I like to talk!

They strolled along a mossy green path,
As Great Grandpa told stories that made him laugh.
He talked about being young again,
And had a wistful look as he remembered back

"Once, when I was little like you,
I got lost in the woods and didn't know what to do."
"Oh, no!" Little Cub said, his eyes wide with fright,
"How did you get home that night?"

"I remembered what my father said,
To follow the river up ahead,
Until there was no place to roam -
That's where my family made their home."

"You see," he continued, as they walked along,
"Your family will always keep you strong.
No matter what surprises come your way,
Your family's advice is there to stay."

Little Cub nodded as he stopped to eat berries,
They were juicy and plump and made him merry.
He was a growing bear, so every food was yummy,
And needed lots of berries to fill his tummy!

Great Grandpa told a funny story about sliding down a hill
In the middle of winter - it was quite a thrill!
Down, down, down, he slid so fast,
Finally landing in a snowdrift at last.

Little Cub giggled at the picture in his mind,
Of Great Grandpa Bear tumbling from behind.
"Why weren't you sleeping?" (It was winter after all.)
Great Grandpa thought about it and tried to recall.

"I knew it was time for a long, long nap,
But I wasn't ready for that winter snap.
So, I went exploring until the very last minute,
Until hibernation set the limit."

"You know what hibernation is, don't you, my boy?"
Little Cub knew the answer and said with joy,
"Yes! It's a season when all bears sleep!
Curled up together in a cave warm and deep."

Hi-ber-na-tion

"That's right!" Great Grandpa said with a yawn.
"I look forward to hibernation all year long."
Little Cub smiled at his Great Grandpa Bear,
Who had wrinkles under his eyes and laugh lines to spare

At last, they slowed down by a bubbling stream,
And took a long drink from the water that gleamed.
Little Cub looked down and saw their reflection,
"Hey, it's us, Grandpa!" he said with affection.

"I see you!" Great Grandpa said with a friendly tease.
"I see you back!" Little Cub replied with ease.
"Oh, how I love you," he said with a splash.
"And I love YOU!" he said tumbling back.

They lay on the grass and looked up at the sky,
Finding shapes in the clouds as they floated by.
Great Grandpa fell asleep for a short power nap -
His snoring made him jump as he heard a loud "clap!"

Little Cub was chasing bees, but got too close,
And one bee stung him right on the nose!
"Ouch!" he said, with tears in his eyes,
But Great Grandpa kissed him and said, "It's alright."

In his Grandpa's embrace, Little Cub found,
A love so great, it knew no bounds.
He knew that his family's roots ran deep,
And all the memories were his to keep.

Finally, it was time for them to head back,
So, they took the same trail - it was easy to track.
Over the hill and down the slope,

Ahh, what a wonderful time they'd had,
Another great day of which they were glad.
They LOVED spending quality time together,
And would cherish these moments forever and ever.

No matter what path Little Cub would take,
He would always give honor for Great Grandfather's sake.
He would carry the family name with pride,
And know he was always on his side.

"Great Grandpa loves me!" he shouted with glee,
As his voice echoed loud and free.
Ge laughed aloud as they rounded the hill,
Saying, "I sure do love you, and I always will."

Made in the USA
Columbia, SC
17 December 2024

49864338R00020